I Know My Daddy Loves Me

Barbara Wolfgram

Illustrated by Marlene McAuley

CPH
Concordia Publishing House

This book is dedicated to Joshua.

Dear Parent,

Reading this book with your children will provide you with a wonderful opportunity to relax and enjoy each other. It expresses the delight and security of children in the knowledge of their father's love. The simple rhyming style and patterned text lend themselves to easy listening and reading. Most of all, the book models language that can be used to articulate to children the love of Jesus.

As you read this book together, take time to listen to your children and share your love with them. Tell them of Jesus' love and help them to know how precious they are in our Lord's eyes. As they feel secure in your love, they will become more and more secure in God's love.

P.S. Be sure to look for the companion book, *I Know My Mommy Loves Me,* also published by Concordia Publishing House.

Each morning when I first awake,
My daddy hugs me. I feel great.

I think my daddy loves me.

He gets me dressed and combs my hair.
He lets me hug my teddy bear.

I think my daddy loves me.

On sunny days we take long walks.
On rainy days we play with blocks.

I think my daddy loves me.

I like it when we take a hike
Or sail along up on his bike.

I think my daddy loves me.

At the park, we swing and play.
I'd like to come here every day.

I think my daddy loves me.

He holds me when we're on the slide.
And then we like to run and hide.

I think my daddy loves me.

It's fun to eat a picnic lunch.
The grapes and chips I like a bunch.

I think my daddy loves me.

My daddy helps me fly a kite.
I hold the string with all my might.

I think my daddy loves me.

Sometimes when I am tired or sick,
He sings to me; I'm better quick.

I think my daddy loves me.

He likes to sit and read with me.
It makes me happy as can be.

I think my daddy loves me.

He reads to me of Jesus' love
And how He came from heaven above.

I think my daddy loves me.

He tells me Jesus loves us all,
No matter if we're big or small.

I think my daddy loves me.

He tells me I am Jesus' lamb,
God's sweet and blessed child I am.

I think my daddy loves me.

And as I go to bed each night,
We say our prayers; he hugs me tight.

I KNOW my daddy loves me.